BEST
FRIENDS
FOREVER

Also by Alexandria Blaelock

SHORT STORY COLLECTIONS
The Histories of Hayward Hall
Lovelorn, Lovestruck and Love at First Sight
Common or Garden Variety Heroes
Case Files of the Wilkinson Detective Agency
Unavoidable Fates
Christmas Travesties
Five Faces of Felicia Clarke
Little Place Called Home
Security Directorate Dossiers v. 1.
Security Directorate Dossiers v. 2.

FICTION
That Love Nonsense
Taipan vs Brown
The Ghost and Ms Cox
Friends Like That
Weaving the Wildwood
Wolf vs Orb

MS BLAELOCK'S BOOKS
Stress Free Dinner Parties
Signature Wardrobe Planning
Holistic Personal Finance
Minimally Viable Housekeeping
Planning a Life Worth Living

PICTURE BOOKS
Australia Felix

SELECTED SHORT STORIES
Alma's Grace
Blood and Bloody Profanity
Cancelled by the Cartel
Dingo Hunting
Honoris Virilis Respectu
Mince Pie Mystery
Remains of Christmas

BEST FRIENDS FOREVER

A FELICIA CLARKE
SHORT STORY

ALEXANDRIA BLAELOCK

BlueMere Books
MELBOURNE, AUSTRALIA

For permission requests, please contact enquiries@bluemerebooks.com.

Ordering Information:
Discounts are available on quantity purchases. For details, contact orders@bluemerebooks.com.

Best Friends Forever/Alexandria Blaelock
paperback ISBN: 978-1-922744-14-2
digital ISBN: 978-1-922744-15-9

Book Layout © BookDesignTemplates.com
Cover Art © Yurii Seleznev via depositphotos

BEST FRIENDS FOREVER

I should really start this story in the beginning. When I first met Felicia rather than at the end when I last saw her, before...

Well, before her funeral.

But given there was a break of about fifty years between the dates, and for forty-five of them, I'd lost contact.

I'd married Danforth, a nice enough man, and he'd taken me back to his home town up North.

I quit work, had a family, and just didn't get around to replying to her last letter.

At the time she was everything I wanted to be.

But after a while, I simply forgot about her.

Now I think back and wonder how that was even possible.

She and I were quite the thing at Mungo's Secretarial College.

Along with...

What's his name?

It's on the tip of my tongue.

T...

Th...

Thad? Theo? Thomas?

Thomas, that was it.

Tom.

I'd always thought she'd marry him, but apparently, her father was a bit of a layabout and her family was as good as destitute while she was growing up and she vowed that she would never be beholden to a man.

Or dependent on a man's...

What was it she called it?

I can't remember, but I do think she really loved him.

Tom, this is.

And anyway, I think she wanted to take care of her mother, and if she got married, she'd have to give up work and take care of her husband.

I tell you; he had the patience of a saint that man.

Such a shame he died of tetanus; I mean who could ever have imagined that?

Awful way to die.

She gave up on God after that - just a bigger, badder man she said.

Perhaps he's waiting for her at the Pearly Gates.

More the fool him then, he'll be waiting for all eternity because she's not going to get there.

Nuts. Just nuts.

Anyway, where was I?

When I got married, I wouldn't say there were fireworks at the beginning, but he's been a good provider and really, what woman could ask for more than that?

So that being said, I did my duty by my husband too.

When he turned his attentions to his secretary, if you know what I mean, I was quite frankly glad to be rid of it.

And when he left me for her it was hilarious.

She was not much older than our daughter, and as you probably know, life with a young woman in the house can be quite turbulent.

Quite frankly, I can't believe he forgot that.

Not to mention that young women these days are somewhat more liberated than us, and he ended up washing both their clothes, cooking food for the two of them and tidying up after her.

I almost felt sorry for him when he came snivelling back to me, though I was under no illusions that he felt anything for me.

Just longed for the calm, easy life I provided him.

So, let's just say we renegotiated the terms of our marriage, and he increased my housekeeping by several thousand and stopped querying my expenditure quite so thoroughly.

Win-win all around, isn't that what they say you should aim for?

And in a way, this was what led me to meeting Felicia again.

I'd packed my big travel handbag with supplies, and we caught the train to London for Danforth's cancer treatment.

And my goodness the whole place was dreary.

Perhaps I've become a Northerner now, but it seemed all gloom to me.

Gloomy London sky, gloomy London hospital, gloomy hospital waiting room.

Perhaps when they're new, waiting rooms are bright and fresh, but after a point, patient fatigue and illness seeps into the walls and floor, coating them with a kind of grey misery.

Or perhaps it's generations of Nurse Ratched live-alikes.

I like to think I have absolutely no psychic ability whatsoever, but even I felt the load on my shoulders gain at least ten stone as I walked through the hospital door.

I sat in the scruffy waiting room and eased my stiff neck by stretching it as far back as I could make it go, then rolled it backwards and forwards against my shoulders.

It was the kind of sore neck you get when you've been hunching your shoulders too long.

The kind of dull throbbing soreness you get when you're stressed out, as the young things like to say.

I tried not to sigh, not to take a deep breath of the refrigerated, recycled and reconditioned air. Perfumed, as it was, with a strange and unpleasant mix of sharp pure alcohol, dirt and antiseptic floor cleaner.

Plus, a hint of urine, if not from Danforth slumping next to me, then presumably someone else in the waiting room.

I have one good eye thanks to cataract surgery last year, and I need a hearing aid, but somehow my sense of smell is sharper than ever.

Had I grown up at a different time, and in France, I'm sure I would've apprenticed as a Nose for a Perfume House instead of attending Mungo's.

Then again, maybe my nose isn't sharper, maybe it's just that I've had more exposure to different scents.

I could probably trace my life through the scents.

Wood polish, old books and cigar smoke when I started work at Father's practise.

Then fresh paper, ink and typewriter ribbons at Mungo's evening classes twice a week.

Fresh mown lawn, lavender and hot dirt when I lost my virginity. To a stranger who smelled of cigarettes, diesel fuel, and sticky date pudding.

Those were the days.

When I was a new adult, unchaperoned, set loose on the world.

I wonder a little bit, what would have become of me if Father had chosen a different secretarial college and I hadn't met Felicia.

I certainly wouldn't have lost my virginity to a stranger, found myself pregnant, or set on Danforth as a suitable father.

Poor Danforth, perhaps he would have met a nicer, kinder woman than me.

Nonetheless, there we were. Three young people (counting Tom), out on the town.

Smoking, drinking, staying out late.

Father didn't approve, said I would come to a bad end, and he was right about that, though not the bad end he was thinking about.

You may not believe it, talking to me now, but I was shy and naive. Everything was new and exciting, and I felt very daring as I eased into my life of duplicity.

Felicia on the other hand was worldly and a bit jaded. I wonder now, what she saw that made her so thoroughly grown up at such a young age.

The way she handled Tom...

Stringing him along all those years.

Though I suppose she strung me along as well.

Felicia glowed with something worldly and cosmopolitan.

Like I imagine the apple that poisoned Sleeping Beauty. Something enticing, seemingly wholesome, and glossy; an enchanting mask hiding the bad seed within.

Who am I kidding - Tom and I, we were both smitten.

She was the one that took us to the club where I met the stranger.

She encouraged me to drink the cocktail the stranger bought me.

She encouraged me to live a little, to dance and kiss the stranger.

And then she left me, taking Tom with her. Left me to the tender ministrations of the stranger.

Whose name I never knew.

How different would my life have been if I had known his name...

And how to contact him.

Still.

You have to move on, don't you?

I used her tricks to snare Danforth.

Stalking him through Father's firm, tricking him into sleeping with me, deceiving him over his paternity (they do say there's one born every minute for a reason).

Allowing him to take the fall with Father for deflowering his daughter.

Quick registry office marriage.

Following him into banishment.

Though moving to his home town did give me the opportunity to create the fiction of love at first sight, a whirlwind romance, happily ever after.

To reinvent myself as a kinder, more understanding woman.

With my own bad seed hidden deeply inside.

So, there I was, in the waiting room with Danforth.

Waiting for a nurse to come get him, and to an extent, waiting for him to die.

When I smelled something like the smell of Mungo's Secretarial College. Fountain pen ink and fresh paper.

Though the nurse called Danforth's name just that minute, and I forgot about it.

Too busy helping him up and supporting him as he walked towards the nurses' station where a male nurse took over and helped him through the door to the treatment room where I could not follow.

And then I was left to my own devices for six hours until it was time to collect him and take him to the hotel I'd booked.

He's always ill that first night so I don't like to take the train straight home.

Besides, I don't enjoy cleaning up the mess, so it's much better when he's closer to a bathroom when he's vomiting or got diarrhoea.

Infinitely so when I don't have to clean it up.

Though I can still smell it.

Usually, I prefer to get a take-out coffee and go to a local park with it. I'll read, do some puzzles, write some letters. Maybe do a little shopping later.

But the London gloom had turned to London rain, and I didn't much want to go out in that, so I ordered a coffee and took it to one of the tables in the hospital cafeteria.

Primed, as it were with the hint of fountain pen ink.

Obviously, something more workmanlike in black or blue-black, than something more feminine in violet or magenta.

I wasn't consciously looking for Felicia, hadn't thought of her for thirty years at least.

But she was sitting at a table in the middle of a sea of empty tables, so she was easy to notice.

Though it kind of felt as though her past had finally caught up with her, and everyone had heard of her, and shunned her by getting up and leaving the cafeteria as soon as she walked in.

She was of course wearing a hat, though not the kind of close skull cap most commonly seen on cancer patients, but a flamboyantly bright forget me not blue cloche with a rather large brown feather stabbed through the folded-up brim.

And who wouldn't notice a woman alone in a room with a look-at-me hat?

Not that I immediately knew it was her, but that the way her neck curved as she wrote in a notebook seemed familiar.

She glanced up as I looked at her, and held my gaze for a moment before looking back at the book she was writing in.

Dismissing me.

As of no consequence.

I don't suppose she recognised me, I look like what I am now; a short, plump, kindly old lady.

Someone's doting grandmother.

But she looked a bit familiar and it took me a moment to see through the years to the woman I'd once known better than I knew myself.

Yes she'd aged, but she was still thin, still sat as upright as if she had a poker up her arse.

See?

I hadn't even spoken to her and already the bad seed was growing like the unwanted weed it was.

Lord knows why I didn't just leave it alone. Why I had to go and ask was she Felicia Clarke.

Why I had to ask how she'd been and what had happened to her in the meantime.

"Dying," she'd said, "three months max."

I sat down, partly the shock of the news, and partly the shock of the delivery.

It seemed she hadn't grown any more subtle in the intervening period.

"I'm sorry," I said, and I really was.

This wasn't the end I'd wanted for her.

Initially, I'd wanted something short and sharp like a stiletto between the ribs.

But it had been a long time, and I had mellowed and come round to thinking that actually, my life had been incredibly lucky.

Blessed with three children in long term relationships, eight grandchildren and two great-grandchildren!

Amazing to see at Christmas time when the kids take care of all the work and I get to be the best granny ever.

None of which would have happened without her.

I asked, "is there anything I can do?"

And of course, she said no.

"Come to my funeral," she added with a sardonic laugh.

So, I spent my six hours waiting with Felicia, or I suppose, more like she waited with me given she'd just heard the news.

"What will you do?" I asked.

"Go up north to be with my niece," she said, evading my eyes.

I laughed, "nice try, what will you really do?"

She smiled, amused I'd caught her in a lie, "you always could see through me. I've booked into a hospice."

I was fairly sure she'd done no such thing; Felicia wasn't one to wait for anything.

Though maybe she'd booked in, but wasn't planning on arriving.

And if that was the case, she wouldn't be telling anyone in case she left a trail the Police could follow and lay charges.

I didn't press her further.

"Why don't we get out of here, go for cocktails and lunch, reminisce about old times?" she asked.

"I'd like that," I replied.

We went to the Savoy Grill, ate an indecently expensive lunch (which she paid for), and drank so many gin and tonics it seemed like I might be the one throwing up later that night.

"Thank you," she said as she left me, "you've cheered me up no end."

Hugging me, which felt a little final given she'd never been a touchy-feely kind of person.

I watched her weaving in and out of the pedestrians on her way to Charing Cross Tube station, wondering whether I should follow her.

Or warn someone.

Though I had no idea who.

She turned and saw me watching her, grinned her old mischievous grin, waved an outlandishly large wave and disappeared around the corner.

I glanced at my watch and realised I was going to have to get my skates on if I was going to get back to the hospital in time to pick up Danforth.

But at that moment, one of the waiters from the restaurant dashed out and pressed her notebook into my hand, gabbling something and dashing back in.

She was long gone, so I shoved it in my bag and forgot about it, and got back to the hospital just in time.

Poor Danforth was as feeling tired and drained as you might expect. We took a cab to the hotel, and I ordered consommé to the room on the off chance he could keep it down.

The next day we went back North, and life settled down again.

It was only a week or so later I saw her death notice in the newspaper over breakfast.

I exclaimed, and Danforth asked what the matter was.

"That girl I was at secretarial college," I said, "Felicia Clarke. She was discovered dead of cancer in her bed last Tuesday."

"She was a wild one," he replied, "I'm surprised she didn't die sooner."

I grunted non-committally, then mentioned I'd seen her that day at the hospital.

"She's being laid to rest next to her mother in Oxford next week. I think I'd like to go."

His turn to grunt non-committally.

"I always knew," he said.

"Knew what?"

"I always knew I wasn't David's father."

My ears were ringing and I felt dizzy as my blood plummeted to the floor.

He lifted the pot to refill my teacup, spooning in a generous teaspoon of sugar, and nudging the saucer towards me.

"I always knew you didn't love me when I married you, but I thought perhaps I loved you enough for both of us Etta."

I opened and closed my mouth a few times, but really, there was nothing to say about that.

"You've been good to me, so I've never breathed a word to anyone. I just wanted you to know you aren't the only one who can keep a secret."

I don't mind telling you my opinion of him went up a thousand-fold.

"I'm sorry," I said. And I meant it.

"It's all in the past now. You'll be attending my funeral soon enough, and perhaps when you do, your tears won't be crocodile tears."

So I packed my travel handbag again and redis-covered Felicia's notebook on the train, looking for my thermos of tea.

I held it in my hands for a long time, trying to decide whether to open it.

It's not like I was particuarly interested in any-thing she had to say.

The train shuddered and I dropped it.

Time slowed down as the pages opened and landed written word up.

The thing is that you can't not read things that are written down. You don't form the intention, it just happens.

So before I'd even picked it up I'd read her notes on drugs and side effects, and come to the conclusion it was her suicide plan.

As I said, she wasn't one for waiting.

So I dropped it in the bin when I changed trains at Brimingham.

Felicia's funeral, was surprisingly well attended for a woman who'd been single all her life and only worked for two people.

And a couple of weeks after that, I attended my husband's.

My poor daughter had dropped in on him while I was away and found him slumped over his breakfast table. She'd called an ambulance, but they couldn't revive him.

They thought it would be best not to tell me until I got back given I was away and there was nothing I could do anyway.

I found that I missed Danforth after he was gone. I may not have loved him when I married him, but I grew fond of him over the years, and he will be sadly missed.

Unlike Felicia.

THE END

As a small token of my thanks for reading...

Please enjoy 10% off everything (excluding shipping)

at alexandriablaelock.com

with the code tom10.

Turn the page for some ideas where to use it,

Do you have what it takes to be a hero?

Whether that's running into a burning building, standing up for what you know is right, or saving the Princess it's going to take everything you've got and more besides.

In this genre-spanning collection of original stories, five women draw on resources they didn't know they had.

Join them, if you dare.

Home is where the heart is

You can struggle to find the place you call home. It's not a place, it's a feeling. You'll know it when you find it.

This collection of short stories explores our search for a place we can call home.

Short, sweet and relatable, these stories will make you homesick for places you've never been.

Welcome to Wilkinson's

I'm afraid Mr Hall's running a little late, can I get you a tea or coffee while you wait?

No?

What if I tell you about some of the recent cases we've been involved in?

Get comfortable and settle in for a wild ride.

you go girl!
The opposite
of winning
isn't losing,
it's quitting.
· Martha Rosette Lutz ·
Time for
a nice cup
of tea and
a sit down
Time for
a nice cup
of tea and
a biscuit

Time for a nice cup of tea
and a sit down
BEWARE THE EMPTINESS GREMLINS

Australian author Alexandria Blaelock writes mostly fantasy and mystery.

She's appeared in the Stringybark Anthology *Crowd Surfing*, *Pulphouse Fiction Magazine*, and *Ellery Queen's Mystery Magazine*.

She's also written five self-help books applying business techniques to personal matters like getting dressed, tidying up, and feeding friends.

Discover more at alexandriablaelock.com.

www.ingramcontent.com/pod-product-compliance
Lightning Source LLC
Chambersburg PA
CBHW051830180726
48283CB00004BA/1373